My First

ABC

Sticker Activity Book

make believe ideas

Have fun exploring this sticker activity book. Use color and stickers to complete the activities. There are also extra stickers to use wherever you want!

Each page focuses on a different letter of the alphabet.
Can you find the animals and objects that begin with each letter?

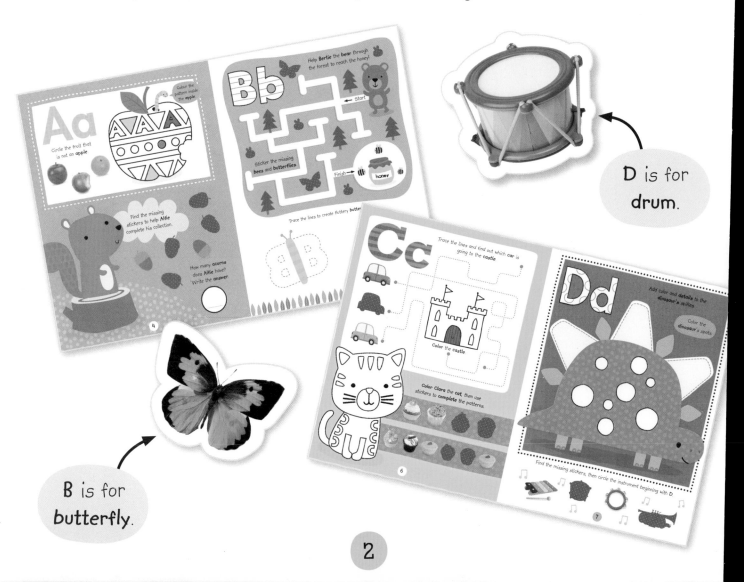

D is for drum.

B is for butterfly.

Some pages include letters hidden in other objects and shapes. You can also find letters in the things around you. How many different letters can you see?

This letter makes the shape of a flower.

This letter makes the shape of two mountains.

You will also find fun press-outs to decorate and use. Complete the press-out door hangers using stickers. Then enjoy playing Pairs or Snap with your press-out game cards.

Have fun!

Aa

Circle the fruit that is not an **apple**.

Color the pattern inside the **apple**.

Find the missing stickers to help **Alfie** complete his collection.

How many **acorns** does **Alfie** have? Write the **answer**.

Bb

Help **Bertie** the **bear** through the forest to reach the honey!

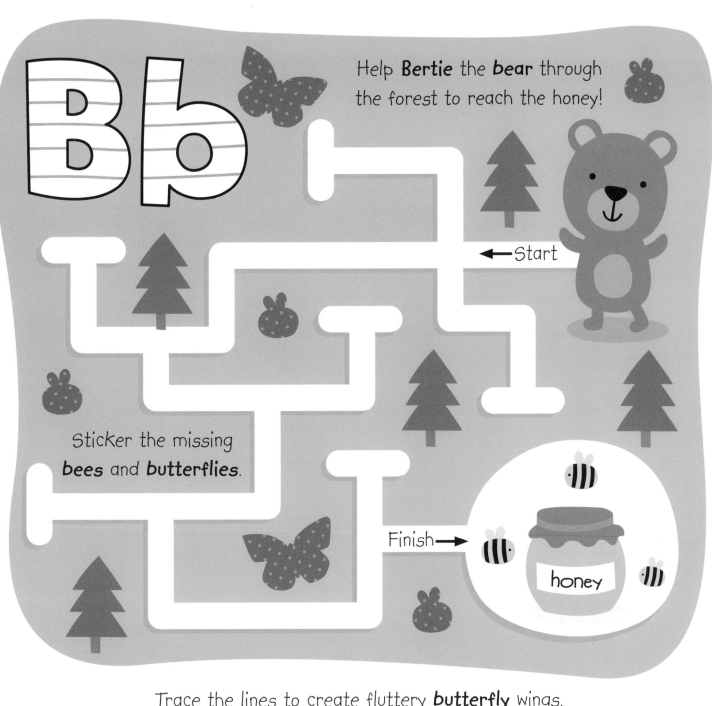

Sticker the missing **bees** and **butterflies**.

Start

Finish

honey

Trace the lines to create fluttery **butterfly** wings.

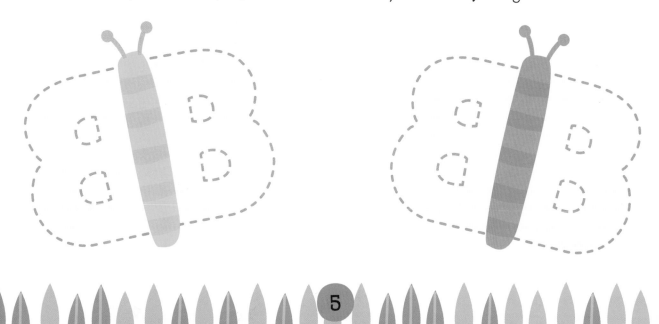

Cc

Trace the lines to find out which **car** is going to the **castle**.

Color the **castle**.

Color **Clara** the **cat**, then use stickers to **complete** the patterns.

Dd

Add **color** and **details** to the **dinosaur's** spikes.

Color the **dinosaur's** spots.

Find the missing stickers, then circle the instrument beginning with **d**.

Ee

Decorate the **elephant** parade with stickers and color!

Can you find the hidden **letters**?

8

Ff

Create **funny faces** using color and stickers. Pay attention to the clues on the photographs!

Shade this space with a pencil, then use an eraser to rub out **fantastic fireworks**.

I have red hair.

I have green glasses.

I have a pink bow.

I have a yellow hat.

I have a blue bow tie.

Fold the page along the dashed line to **find** the **flower**.

Gg

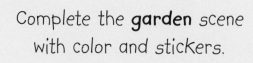

How many birds can you count? Write the answer.

Color the flowers **growing** in the **garden**.

The **garden gnomes** are fishing.
Trace the lines to see who has caught the fish.

Find the missing stickers.

GREEN

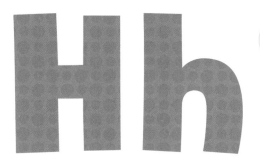

Hh

Use the grids to **help** you draw
the other **half** of each picture.
Finish the pictures by adding color.

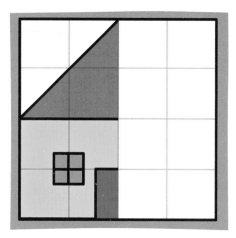 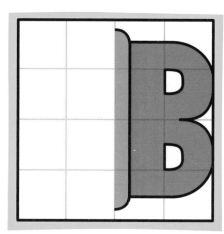 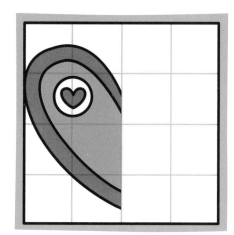

Sticker more **houses** on the **hill**. Point to the **hidden h**.

Use stickers to solve the problems.

2 + 2 =

2 - 1 =

12

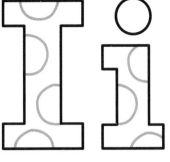

Ii

Sticker toppings on the **ice-cream** cone.

Find stickers to complete the **ice-cream** patterns.

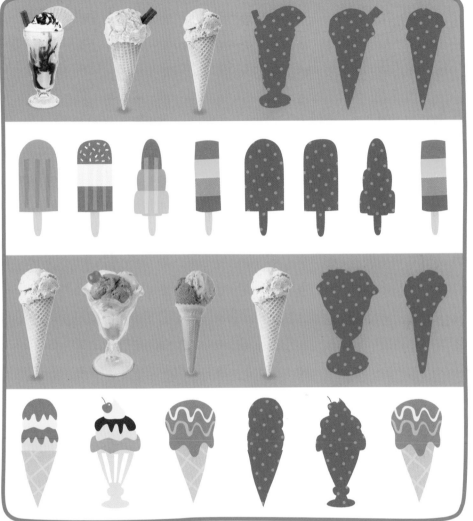

Can you circle five differences between the pictures below?

13

Jj

Add stickers to the **jungle** scene, then use wild colors to finish it!

How many **jaguars** can you count? Write the answer.

Kk

Find the **king** a shiny crown to wear.

Color the picture using the **key** below.

1   2   3   4   5   6

Sticker bows on the **kite's** tail.

Ll

Use the **ladders** to help **Larry** the **lion** reach the top of the **lighthouse**.

How many seagulls can you count? Write the answer.

Start →

Mm

Millie the **mouse** is camping. Look at the list below. Can you find everything in the picture?

Point to the hidden **m**.

2 **m**ountains   I **m**oon   I **m**ouse   2 **m**arshmallows   I glass of **m**ilk

Find the missing stickers to match the **noises** to the correct animals.

How many horseshoes
can you count?
Write the answer.

Oo

Find the missing stickers, then draw lines to match the **opposites**.

cold

Oscar

inside

short

hot

tall

slow

Oscar

outside

fast

20

Build a food machine with color and stickers.
Circle the food that begins with an **o**.

Point to the food that looks like an **o**.

Draw your favorite food **on** the plate.

21

Pp

Decorate the **picture** with color and stickers, then draw a **playful pet** in the frame.

My **pet's** name: ....

Sticker a ball
for the **puppy**.

Sticker a kitten
on the cushion.

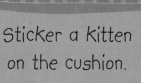

Sticker a carrot
for the rabbit.

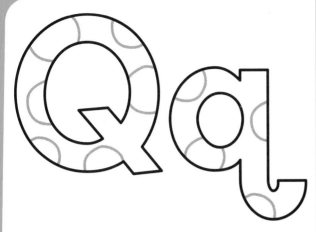

Find the missing stickers, then circle the answer to each **question** in the **quiz**.

What do you wear on your feet?

sunglasses

shoes

hat

Which animal lives in water?

cat

guinea pig

fish

squirrel

Which animal can fly?

mouse

bird

hamster

What grows in the ground?

candy

potatoes

ice cream

cupcake

Rr

Find the missing stickers to help **Ryan** the **robot** build a **rocket**.

How many **red** gears does **Ryan** have? Write the answer.

24

Decorate the scene with color and stickers.

25

S s

Help **Sarah** make a **sand castle** at the **seaside**. Use bright colors and **stickers**.

Use **stickers** to complete the **shell** patterns.

Tt

The **toys** are having a fancy **tea** party. Finish the scene using color and stickers. Then **trace** the **trails** to see which **toy** has eaten a cupcake.

Toys

Uu

Trace the lines to create **umbrellas**.

Shade this storm cloud with a pencil, then **use** an eraser to rub out some raindrops.

Help Rosie the rabbit through the **underground** maze to find her rabbit friend.

Start

Finish

Sticker and doodle funny faces on the **vegetables**.

Trace the lines to find out who reaches the **van**.

Victor

Veronica

Vickie

Simon the spider is making a **web**. Fill the page with **wiggly** doodles.

Sticker **wobbly** things in the **web**.

X x

X marks the spot! Use color and stickers to complete the treasure map, then draw a path through the ocean to help the ship reach the x.

Start

Find a pirate hat for me to wear.

Yy

Use stickers and color to fill the page with **yellow** things.

Can **you** reach the star in the middle of the **yo-yo** maze?

Start

Z z

Draw stripes on the **zebras**, then use stickers to complete the **zoo**.

penguins

giraffe

elephant

lions

Use color and stickers to fill the frames.

Create a pretty flower garden with stickers and color.

Trace the hidden **letters**.

Add color to complete the patterns.

Decorate the **alphabet** superhero with stickers and color.

Point to the hidden **letters**.

Use stickers and doodles to fill
this page with **letter** monsters.

Finish the clothesline using color and stickers.

Point to the hidden **letters**.

How many socks are on the clothesline? Write the answer.

Trace the uppercase and lowercase a's.

A is for apple.

Color the things beginning with **a**.

These pages are packed with fun coloring activities!

alien

alligator

apple

acorns

ant

B is for bear.

Color the things beginning with **b**.

bee

butterfly

bus

birds

bear

banana

ball

boots

40

Trace the uppercase and lowercase c's.

C is for cat.

Color the things beginning with c.

cloud

cars

crown

cupcake

caterpillar

carrot

crab

cat

41

D is for dinosaur.

Color the things beginning with **d**.

dolphin

dragonfly

dog

dessert

donut

dinosaur

daisy

42

Trace the uppercase and lowercase *e*'s.

E is for elephant.

Color the things beginning with **e**.

elephants

eight eggs

envelope

Trace the uppercase and lowercase f's.

F is for flower.

Color the things beginning with f.

fly

fox

forest

flower

frog

fish

Trace the uppercase and lowercase g's.

G is for garden.

Color the things beginning with **g**.

garden

grass

gnome

grapes

giraffe

Trace the uppercase and lowercase h's.

H is for house.

Color the things beginning with h.

hot-air balloon

helicopter

hat

houses

huge hen

Trace the uppercase and lowercase i's.

I is for igloo.

Color the things beginning with i.

icy
snowflakes

igloo

insect

ice-cream cones

J is for jungle.

Color the things beginning with j.

jellyfish

jaguar

jungle

Jell-O

Trace the uppercase and lowercase k's.

K is for kite.

Color the things beginning with k.

kite

kangaroo

kitten

king

Trace the uppercase and lowercase l's.

L is for lion.

Color the things beginning with l.

ladybug

laundry

lollipop

leaf

lion

lady

Trace the uppercase and lowercase m's.

M is for moon.

Color the things beginning with m.

moon

mountains

mouse

milk

monkey

Trace the uppercase and lowercase n's.

N is for nest.

Color the things beginning with n.

night

nest

notes

newt

Trace the uppercase and lowercase **O**'s.

O is for octopus.

Color the things beginning with **o**.

owl

oranges

octopus

Trace the uppercase and lowercase p's.

P is for pig.

Color the things beginning with p.

planet

penguin

party

pig

parrot

peacock

Trace the uppercase and lowercase q's.

Q is for queen.

Color the things beginning with q.

QUIZ

quiz

queen

quilt

quail

Trace the uppercase and lowercase r's.

R is for robot.

Color the things beginning with r.

rocket

rain

robot

river

rabbit

Trace the uppercase and lowercase s's.

S is for snail.

Color the things beginning with s.

sun

seagull

sock

spider

squirrel

snail

shell

strawberries

Trace the uppercase and lowercase t's.

T is for train.

Color the things beginning with **t**.

train

tree

tractor

tiger

teapot

table

tortoise

teddy bear

Trace the uppercase and lowercase **u**'s.

U is for umbrella.

Color the things beginning with **u**.

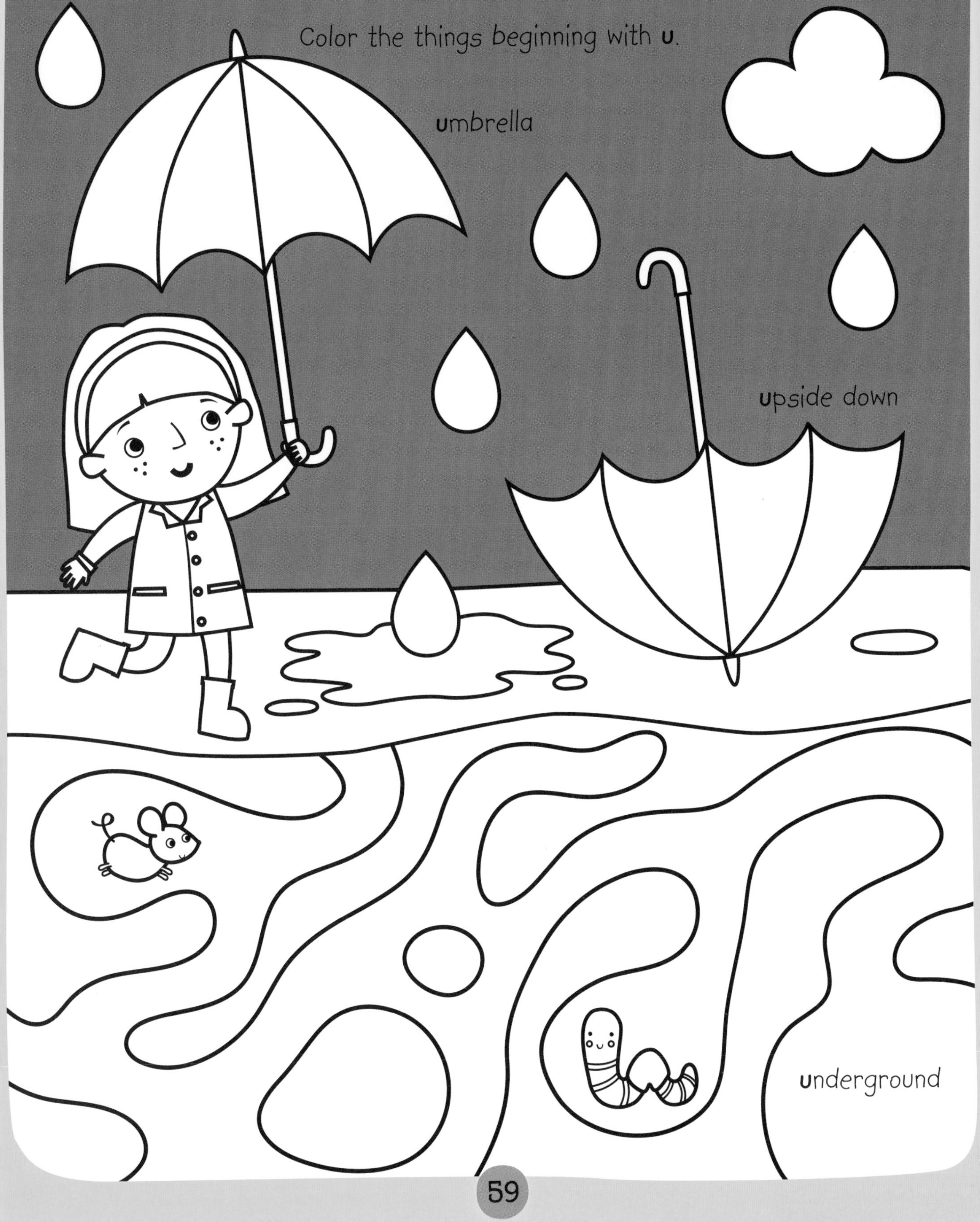

umbrella
upside down
underground

Trace the uppercase and lowercase v's.

V is for van.

Color the things beginning with v.

violet

van

vet

vegetables

Trace the uppercase and lowercase w's.

W is for worm.

Color the things beginning with w.

web

wheels

window

worm

whale

Trace the uppercase and lowercase x's.

X is for xylophone.

Color the things beginning and ending with x.

xylophone

TOYS

toy box

six

62

Trace the uppercase and lowercase y's.

Y is for yo-yo.

Color the things beginning with y.

yak

yo-yo

yogurt

Trace the uppercase and lowercase z's.

Color the things beginning with z.

zoo

zebra